Earth vs The Lava Spiders

Candace Nola

Uncomfortably Dark Horror

Copyright © 2022 by Candace Nola

All rights reserved.

No portion of this book may be reproduced in any form without written permission from the publisher or author, except as permitted by U.S. copyright law.

Published by Uncomfortably Dark Horror.

Edited by 360 Editing (a division of Uncomfortably Dark Horror).

Editors: Candace Nola. Mort Stone.

Cover Art by Grim Poppy Design

Uncomfortably Dark Horror is owned and operated by Candace Nola

Contents

Dedication	V
1. Fever	1
2. Shake, rattle, and roll	3
3. Great Balls of Fire!	7
4. Blueberry Hill	11
5. Lucille	17
6. Jailhouse Rock	25
7. Oh, What A Night!	31
8. What'd I Say?	35
9. Good golly, Miss Molly!	43
Epilogue	49
Afterword	50

This story is dedicated to my usual suspects, the kitty, the puddin', and the sir. To my mom. To Charity. To Bear.

To my writer tribe, Rowland, Mike, Eric, Ruthann, Dan, Carver, Aron, Nikolas, and so many others.

To Judith, for the incredible project idea, and to Lucas, for joining us for this fun foray into the 50's.

To my editors and reviewers, Mort Stone, and Dark Rose, and all of those that help to support and encourage the writing community, all of those that review, host podcasts, hold book tours, and ceaselessly promote and share our work.

To the readers, without you, none of this is possible.

Chapter 1

Fever

Pine Grove, CA. 1958.

"Come on, Gwen, just a peek." Billy whined, pulling his girlfriend Gwen closer to him in the backseat. His athletic good looks were on prominent display, his dark hair styled to perfection with one rebellious curl hovering just over one eye added a hint of bad boy charm to his rakish grin.

"No, Billy. Stop. Good girls don't do those things." Gwen said, trying to pull away from his embrace.

"Good girls don't go to Lover's Lane," Billy said snidely, trying to snake his hand down the front of her sweater again. His face was flushed with arousal and a hint of rising anger.

"I said 'stop,' Billy. I mean it. I didn't know we were going here. You asked if I wanted to see something far out. We should get back to the others, anyway." She tugged away from him and pulled her sweater tightly around her ample bosom. She grabbed for the door handle and opened it, getting out in one fluid motion, then slammed the door of the cherry red rag top behind her.

"Fuuuuccckk..." Billy groaned, slouching angrily in the back seat, slapping one hand down on the leather in frustration. Finally, he followed Gwen out of the car and went to where she leaned against the wooden fence, looking down at the bonfire on the beach.

Their friends were there, outlined against the roaring blaze and night sky, doing the latest dance craze around the fire, beer bottles in hand while they gyrated to the music blaring from the car parked nearby. Faint laughter could be heard over the crashing of the waves.

"I'm sorry, Gwen. I just get so excited being so close to you. I just want to see how beautiful my girl is. Is that so wrong?" He cajoled her, wrapping his arm around her waist, gently this time.

"It is when I ask you to stop." She said primly. "We've only been going steady for two months. Don't you think you're rushing things?" She glared at him then, turning her eyes from the party below.

"Aww. Stop being such a wet rag. All your friends are doing it, that and more, from what the fellas are saying." Billy exclaimed, letting her go and storming to the rag top. "Get in. I'll take you back to the beach, then I'm burning rubber back to the pad."

Gwen glared at his back for a moment before she turned in a huff and got in the car. Billy revved the Chevy as he peeled out of the dirt lane and headed toward the beach, eager to be free of Miss Goodie-two-shoes.

Chapter 2

Shake, rattle, and roll

STRANGE LIGHTS APPEARED OVER Shasta Bay as they drove onto the rocky trail leading to the beach.

"What is that, Billy?" Gwen asked, peering up at the sky through the windshield.

"What's what?" He snapped, both hands angrily gripping the wheel, not bothering to look at her.

"That, Billy, look at the island, those lights. I've never seen that before." She pointed; her voice filled with curious trepidation.

"Big deal, bunch of lights," he scoffed. "Don't be such a spaz, Gwen. It's nighttime. Probably shooting stars or something."

Suddenly, a bright flash lit the sky up like the Fourth of July and a massive explosion shattered the silence. Billy slammed down on the brakes, causing the car to fishtail violently as he struggled with the wheel. A string of curse words left his mouth as the car careened to a stop.

Gwen pointed a shaking hand towards the beach as a rain of ash covered their friends as they huddled down next to their cars.

"What's going on, Billy" she asked, fear coating her voice, making it sound sexier, almost husky.

"I don't know. We better go see." Billy fumbled for the car door, yanking it open, and hauled Gwen out behind him. She came quickly with no protest, one hand automatically covering her nose and mouth as they headed into the shower of ash.

Before they reach the others, a low vibration began beneath their feet and a deep rumbling, like a freight train, fills the air. They froze in their tracks, Billy clutching Gwen to him as she trembled in terror. Twenty yards away, their friends yell for them to get down. Billy pulled Gwen down to the sand with him and covered her with his body the best he could as the beach lurched and roiled under them. The noise was deafening, making their teeth ache as their skulls filled with pressure. Billy slapped both hands over his ears, his mouth open in a silent scream of pain as the pressure mounted.

Just as the pressure dissipated, the sky lit up once more. A frenzied green light show began shooting up from the small hillside on the island, morphing to deep orange spurts of flame that launched into the sky from the top of the smoking hill. Huge fireballs shot from the gaping maw of the mountain and splash down into the sea. Lava bubbled over and poured down the sides. Thick and steaming, the magma rushed over the rocks and plant life, destroying an entire ecosystem in seconds as it spilled into the sea.

The drunk and scared teens crawled to their cars, scrambling on all fours as the churning sea pounded the shore. More explosions sounded from behind them as they struggled to stand and gain traction over the living beach as it undulated beneath them, like it was suddenly alive and chasing them. They reached Billy's car, the only car on somewhat stable ground, and piled in. Six terrified teens screamed all at once, urging Billy to start the car.

Suddenly, it all went quiet, like someone had flipped a switch. The sandy beach settled. The rumbling stopped. Nothing left except the steaming hiss of the pouring lava as it meets the sea, far from the shore. They stopped screaming and stared at the boiling volcano, shock and fear etched on every perfectly tanned face. Then Doris screamed. The others join her as their eyes locked on to what she's already seen.

Chapter 3

Great Balls of Fire!

Down the side of the newly exploded volcano, faster than the lava could go, massive balls of fire were speeding down the mountain. Several had reached the sea, but instead of drowning in a hiss of steam, they bounced and rolled across the waves toward the shore. They could see something dark protruding from the fireballs. Stick-like appendages moved like propellers across the surf.

Billy rocked the ignition forward once more, and the Buick Skylark caught and shot forward, his foot already on the gas. The kids screamed with the sudden motion of the car and the onslaught of terror racing toward them. The Skylark fishtailed around the bonfire, sending sand flying in a dust cloud, before Billy gained control and aimed for the rocky path. Gwen and Doris were screaming beside him, both jammed into the front seat, hands over their mouths as they stared across the beach.

Cliff clung tight to Doris; his hands wrapped around her torso, trying to keep her from falling over the side as they raced along. His face was red from fear and beer, and he was close to puking all over Doris as they sped away from the beach.

The screaming went up in pitch as one of the giant balls slammed into the rear bumper, knocking the car into another skid. Billy gripped the wheel, cussing louder than the girl's screams as he struggled to keep the Skylark from wiping out.

"Go faster, man," Cliff yelled, terror clear on his face as he looked behind them. Doris had her arms locked around Gwen's neck, the two of them shaking in fear. Shock had clouded their senses as the fireball unfolded behind them.

"Billy!" Gwen shrieked just as Walt turned around in the backseat, kneeling on the bench to see better.

"Billy!" She screamed again.

"What? What?! I can't go any faster!" He yelled, barely sparing her a glance, but then he looked in the rearview and the car slowed as his foot went slack, his full focus now on the horror in his rearview.

Four of the flaming balls were right behind them. Two unfolded and took shape as the black appendages extended and bent at various joints. Panic set in as the car stopped with a shuddering jerk.

Giant flaming spiders stood behind the rag top. Lava slid over their body as thick black legs covered in needle-like points sent them skittering along the path. Red eyes glowed on bulbous heads; multiple stalks waved in all directions as the eyes stared at everything all at once. The bodies glowed orange flame, oozing with lava, visible in gaps through its skeletal structure.

Billy felt his pants grow warm but did not bother to look down. The seat of his pants had grown damp minutes ago when both Doris and Gwen had wet themselves in fear, watching the creatures unfurl to their full height.

Walt and Cliff stared, mouths agape, but no words issued forth. Four of the fireballs skittered along the side of the car and rose from the sand, limbs and eyestalks protruding as they reached full mass. Molten lava scorched the side of the Skylark as the spiders surrounded the vehicle. The screaming began anew as Clint's head vanished in a spray of blood and gore. The stump of his head sprayed crimson all over Doris and Gwen, coating them in red. Billy's body lay twitching in the driver's seat with his head and one arm missing; blobs of lava burned through his thighs and stomach as it dripped from the spider fervently chomping on his limbs.

A new spider pounced on the trunk of the car, relieving Walt of his screaming noggin with a loud squelching as his neck separated from his torso. A coarsely barbed leg hastily pulled Walt's body from the seat, skewering him under the ribcage and pulling it to the gore-coated sand. A tug-of-war began between three of the hungry creatures as they gnashed their fanged maws on his appendages, tugging and pulling flesh from his body as they chewed. Blood spurted from their massive jaws and dripped from their smoldering bodies.

A shrill screaming filled the air as one ripped Doris from Gwen's grasp. A huge spider hovered over the side of the car, its front legs piercing Doris as it hauled her upright, spun her body quickly with its legs, wrapping her in shimmering orange mist before it popped her into its hungry mouth like a tootsie roll.

Gwen sat in shock, eyes glazed over, her pale skin coated in gore. It dripped from her like paint, soaked into her hair and her pedal pushers, slithered between her breasts, thick with bits of tissue and brain matter. Her mouth opened, but no sound came out, just a low whimper, fear strangled by terror and lack of oxygen. Her misery did not last long as a blob of lava fell from the orifice of the creature above her and splattered onto her upturned face, bursting her eyeballs from the heat, as it began its slow sizzling descent over her delicate features, eroding them in a haze of melted flesh.

More skittering fireballs poured past the stranded car, now blood red instead of cherry, and raced toward town, leaving the bloody beach behind, covered in a shimmering haze of delicate orange webs.

Chapter 4

Blueberry Hill

THE SPIDERS SCURRIED UP the path toward the main street, poured onto the sidewalks, and burst from alleyways. Gobs of molten lava plopped from them, scorching the asphalt, cars, and storefronts they passed. Their eye stalks danced crazily atop their boiling torso, scanning the area for fresh meat as they propelled their flaming masses through the town. A half-dozen of the creatures launched themselves through the glass window of the diner and began devouring the soda jerk and the waitress that were still there, stuck on cleaning detail before they left for the night. The young people barely had time to scream before lava-filled maws were crunching eagerly on their flesh-covered heads. The slight pop of their eyeballs bursting from the heat could be heard just as the razor-sharp teeth severed their heads from their spine.

Blood arced across the soda fountain and covered the gleaming chrome and Formica countertop. The jukebox dripped crimson rivulets as it played "Ain't It A Shame" by Fats Domino. The headless body of the server toppled over into the nearest leather booth, just before more spiders tore her limbs from her body and gobbled by the smoldering infernos of death.

Two of the creatures bounded through the shattered front window and pounced onto the hood of a Cadillac fleeing down the street, a trio of spiders in hot pursuit. The driver screamed, over-corrected the wheel, and crashed right into Dixon's Drugs on the corner. He tried to scramble away from his open door, but barely touched the sidewalk before they bowled over his body and turned into a gooey snack for two of the flaming arachnids. Within minutes, nothing was left but a dark puddle of gore on the sidewalk and his dark brown penny loafers.

A bright red fire truck roared down the street, sirens screaming, as a dozen flaming arachnids bounded after it. It careened into the side of the town hall as a trio of the creatures landed on its hood, smashing through the windshield, and ripping the screaming man from his seat. The other firefighter leapt from the burning vehicle and went running for shelter. His flight only lasted seconds as the dozen behind them unfurled, bounded, and chomped massive jaws around limbs and heads. They tore the fireman to bloody shreds in minutes, leaving a crimson pool of carnage around the ruined firetruck.

A police car rounded the corner, another close behind it, sirens blaring as their flashing red and blues strobed against the dark street. Spiders surrounded both cars as they fled up the street, desperate to get out of town. A loud screeching sounded as the first car went up on two wheels, scraping along a signpost, as skittering balls of flame topped it over. It skidded on its side before coming to a stop. The man inside screamed as the spiders poured over it, smashing glass and tearing off doors, to get at the tasty human treat inside.

The second car raced past the first, not bothering to stop for his stranded colleague. His mouth was open in a horrified scream as he gripped the wheel with both hands, knuckles white, face red. A stream of curse words emanated from his mouth as he tore down the street, pulverizing what remained of the prior victims. Blood sprayed up and coated the undercarriage of the police car with every half-masticated body part he ran over. Two boulder-sized spiders barreled into the side of the car, sending it flying off course into the ditch.

The car tilted on one side, trapping the man in the driver's seat, the door wedged into the lower part of the trench. Tears poured down his face as he could only watch thick barbed legs punctured the windshield, skewered him right through his doughy jowls, and yanked him through the jagged glass. His spine shattered and folded in half as the creature bit down on his middle, effectively cutting off his screams with a meaty chomp.

Screaming emanated from the few shops along the main street that still had the misfortune to contain warm bodies. The scurrying creatures were everywhere, flames shooting from their bizarrely skeletal bodies, lava dripping down their thickly barbed legs, and razor-sharp teeth crunched and gnashed on wailing women and flailing men. No one got away from the dozens of red eyes that scanned everywhere all at once, while staring directly at their next meal.

Before an hour had passed, Main Street was a river of blood and a trail of smoking asphalt led from town, up through the pine trees to Blueberry Hill, the local drive-in. They left filaments of delicate orange drifting through the treetops and glistening from bushes and shrubs.

The drive-in was packed. Almost every spot in the small clearing was full of cars, rag-tops, pickups, and horny teens. The smell of melted butter and popcorn was thick in the air, followed by the scent of hot dogs and toasted buns. A line of teens stood outside the concession stand in the middle of the lot, eagerly waiting for their turn to order before the next movie started. On the big screen, a clever little commercial played with dancing fountain drinks and hot dogs, enticing customers to go get a snack during intermission.

Several cars rocked on their springs in the darker back rows, their occupants already engaged in a private intermission of their own, trying their hand at the backseat bingo, or rounding second base, or maybe third. An intoxicating scent is in the air, oversexed teenage hormones, pheromones, pizza, and popcorn. The fireballs fixated on the aroma as they launched from the tree line. They left behind small fires in the branches and underbrush as their flaming bodies unfurled mid-air and landed, already biting and tearing at the closest warm body they saw.

The giant creatures spread throughout the clearing like a tidal wave, scurrying and skittering over cars, blankets, and buildings. Screams of terror start as a low murmur then build to a deafening crescendo as the invasion begun.

Spike-covered legs poke holes in leather seats and ragtops. The barbs puncture tin, steel, and wood as they tear through buildings and cars alike, seeking and eating, eating, and seeking. Blood arced across the fleeing teens as they ran frantically between the rows, searching for shelter. The movie screen came alive with sound and motion as "The Blob," the night's second hit feature, played. The writhing mass of smoldering skittering creatures feasted on lava-roasted eyeballs and thrashing bodies of all shapes and sizes as the monstrous Blob grew ever larger on screen with each victim it consumes.

Dozens of the spiders stalk their prey, staking their barbed limbs into fleeing backs, tanned stomachs, and soft necks, wrenching writhing bodies from beneath the cars and down from tree limbs. A thick moist sound filled the air, much like the uncomfortable squelching of pasta salad being stirred too fast, as the boulder-sized arachnids consumed their prey. Blood pooled on the ground, shimmering red-black puddles that reflected the glowing eyes above them.

Blueberry Hill burned, the scent of roasted flesh, copper, and pine hung heavy in the air. The last of the screaming faded as the creatures gathered as one, eye stalks twisting and turning, before they set off rolling and scurrying through the trees once more, trailing glowing fibers behind. The hunt was not yet over, a fresh scent driving them on.

As the creatures vacated the blood-soaked clearing, a sudden frantic popping noise burst into existence, like a million BB Guns all being shot at once. The popcorn kernels in the burning concession stand have exploded into crispy white puffs that quickly fall into puddles of ash and gore.

Chapter 5

Lucille

"Gary!" Delores Smithers called to her husband from the kitchen.

"Yes, dear?" came his quiet reply from the den, just beyond her line of sight.

"Do you smell smoke?" She called out again, drying her hands on the faded dish towel and smoothing her skirt down as she headed down the short hall to the den.

Gary turned to look at her when she entered, a warm smile on his face. He folded the newspaper in half and set it aside before he replied.

"Smoke? I don't think so. Why do you ask?"

"Yes, like wood smoke. It's coming from outside somewhere. Come to the kitchen."

He sighed and slipped his feet into his slippers once more.

"I'm sure it's nothing, dear." he said, but followed her anyway.

The pair entered the kitchen and stood near the sink, watching the curtains flutter over the small open window. The sharp acrid scent of burning wood and green vegetation filled the air, marked with something deeper and meatier somehow. It's a scent that makes Gary wrinkle his nose.

"What is that?" Delores asked, sniffing, then peering harder out of the small window, a faint glow appearing sporadically in the distance.

"Let me look outside." her husband replied, glancing at the weird glimmers of light that seem to flicker in the night sky.

"I'm not sure you should. Why don't you just call Sheriff Whitman?"

Gary looked back at her with one eyebrow raised. "And say what? That you saw strange lights? I at least need to know what is going on if I am to call anyone, don't you agree?" Turning back to the hallway, he headed toward their front door.

"Stay here." He called out over his shoulder as he disappeared.

Delores was already on the phone, dialing the sheriff. Her gut is churning something fierce, and her skin has dimpled with gooseflesh. Something is wrong. She can feel it.

Gary pulled the door open and stood on the front porch, hands on his hips as he surveyed his front lawn and those of his neighbors. Tidy squares of grass glistened in front of each well-kept house along their cul-de-sac. Smooth driveways lead to garages where family cars and bikes are kept. A proper mailbox stands in front of each house, to the left of every driveway, and white picket fences separate each lawn, keeping cats, dogs and wandering toddlers safe.

Gary sighed in utter contentment. This was a good neighborhood, full of good people, and nice houses. He again congratulated himself on choosing to move the family here. His job at the car lot was going well, and he was one of their top salesmen.

Nodding in agreement with his inner monologue, he trotted down the steps and followed the pristine sidewalk to the street. Stopping for a moment, he stood there, peering into the sky just over the tree line where the lights had been. An odd rumbling noise teased his ear, faint and low, almost as if his stomach was growling. He grew quiet and listened harder, trying to place the sound.

He turned to his left, looking toward Blueberry Hill, breathing as quietly as possible as he spotted the lights bouncing along through the trees like a dozen flashlights hovering in the branches. *No, not flashlights*, he thought. *That was wrong.* These lights were small bursts of red, with an orange glow following beneath. They moved rapidly, blinking in and out of existence as he watched. Gary couldn't track any one light for longer than a second at a time. The chaotic motion was making his head hurt and his nose had started to run from the smoke and the overpowering scent of burning rot and wood.

His stomach clenched, as did his sphincter, and he shuffled backward, toward his house, toward safety. Something was wrong with whatever this was, something bad was happening. He felt the fine hairs on the back of his neck rise and gooseflesh cropped up on his arms. His bowels turned to water as the lights neared the edge of the trees. Suddenly, he was positive that he did not want to see. He ran for the house, nearly knocking Delores over as he vaulted up the steps. He grabbed her by one arm and yanked her into the house, slamming the door over her protests, locking it before he took a breath.

"What on earth is the matter with you?" She exclaimed. "What's happening?"

Gary bent forward, hands on his knees, panting hard, shaking his head at her questions.

"Gary, for Chrissakes, talk to me!"

"Bad." He huffed, "whatever it is, it's bad. Get in the basement, now!"

"The basement?" Delores shrilled, "What on earth for?"

"Delores!" Gary stood and began dragging her to the basement door. "Get. In. The. God. Damned. Basement. NOW!" He threw the door open and pointed. "Go!"

Delores stared at him for a long moment, then finally clomped her way down the stairs. "There better be a good reason for this, Gary."

"Just stay quiet and hide. I'll be down in a minute." Gary closed the door behind her and then rushed back to the kitchen window to peer out.

"What in the world is going on?" He exclaimed, watching the burning boulders bounce down the street. There were several black and pointed branches sticking out of each one. He shook his head. *No. That's not possible*. The sticks were moving, propelling the balls along somehow.

He backed away as three of the massive orbs veered off course and toward his lawn. NO!

Not Lucille!

He raced through the kitchen, flung open the back door, and raced for the garage door. His brand-new Cadillac sat just inside. Gleaming under the lights, chrome sparkling like crystal, leather seats in pristine condition. His pride and joy, fresh off the lot. He had worked for this car. He dashed inside the garage and rounded the rear of Lucille, hefting the old ball bat from the corner as he raised the large door.

Nothing was getting past him. Not tonight.

He stood ready, at the top of the driveway, bat braced in his hands, his body falling into the familiar stance. Years of Little League had conditioned him, and those skills followed him through college. Best years of his life, baseball games, peanuts, and trophies. He loved the sport, but he loved Lucille more. He stared down the giant balls of flame as they spun across his lawn, scorching the freshly mown grass.

He almost lowered the bat, as his jaw dropped open, watching the orb ricochet off his front steps and stop. Stick-like propellers slowed their movements as it hovered there. The grass smoldered beneath it as two more joined it, slowly spinning in place, and then stopped.

Gary felt his bladder let go as the trio unfurled from their torsos and rose to full height. Flames burst from the bony black frame, lava slid down the eight limbs and plopped to the ground. Eight eyestalks bounced up on its head and began scanning and rotating in all directions.

"What the fuck?" Gary exclaimed, hefting the bat once more, feet squishing in his wet slippers as he faced the biggest damn spiders he had ever seen.

Suddenly, they bounded toward him, and he shrieked but held firm.

THWACK!

Gary swung with all his might.

SQUEEEEEE! SQUEEEEEE!

The creature squealed as he knocked it off course. Gary swung again.

THWACK! THWACK!

Two more hits connected, even as the other two creatures advanced. Gary stepped back toward Lucille, feeling his hip connect with her bumper. He stopped and dropped into his swinging stance once more.

SQUEEEEEEE!

They pounced as if on cue! The trio of arachnids landed right on Lucille, lava plopping down their legs and flames licking at the leather seats, and on the hood where they stood, swaying. A haze of orange swirled out from beneath the creatures. A delicate webbing drifted through the garage, coating Gary and Lucille, burning where it landed.

Gary howled in fury. GET OFF LUCILLE! GET OFF HER, NOW!

He swung, again and again, spit and cuss words flying from his mouth in equal amounts.

SQUEEEEEEE! SQUEEEEEEE! SQUEEEEEEE!

Every swing connected with a burning spider part, landing solidly on their legs and bodies, but nothing seemed to take them down. Their bodies were massive and strong, even if they resembled the skeleton of a spider rather than an actual organic body. Lava dripped with every motion and poured over Lucille, charring her body, her seats, her paint, her whitewalls.

Gary howled as if in physical pain. Fury, not fear, driving his attack as he went after the creatures in a frenzy, trying to save his car; all thought of his wife alone in the house were far from his mind. He swung again and again, until finally, he was backed into a corner. The spiders advanced on hissing and spitting fire. Lava oozed from their bodies as he screamed.

"LUCILL–."

The biggest of the spiders slammed its mouth down over Gary's screaming head, severing it from his neck, as Lucille sat in ruins behind them. The other two made fast work of devouring Gary's twitching torso as it slumped to the garage floor. Blood inched toward the drain in the floor as their gaping mouths consumed Gary's body.

Delores sat on the bottom step, trembling, as a horrible racket sounded from outside the house. She heard Gary screaming his fool head off about his car. Lucille. She snorted and shook her head. What kind of grown man names his car? And here she was, sat alone in the basement, scared to death, while he was worried about a damn car? She was going to give him a piece of her mind, just as soon as whatever the hell was going on out there was over.

CRASH! CRASH! CRASH!

She jumped up, startled, eyes wide and staring up toward the basement door. One hand went to her throat, clutching her dainty string of pearls. She was never without them. That would never do. Grandma would roll over in her grave to see a lady without her pearls on. Delores gasped, her hand moving up to cover her mouth.

CRASH! CRASH! CRASH!

The house shook over her head and an enormous THUD sounded as something fell. *Oh, no. No. No. No.* Delores shook her head, over and over, like a dog worrying at a chew toy. She backed away from the steps, frightened, watery eyes never leaving the door. Whatever *it* was, *was* in the house.

She inched closer toward the back wall, where the basement door led out to the yard. She could go out that way, get Steve, and get the hell away from here. She hoped Lucille was okay enough to drive, despite her feelings on its name. She smelled smoke stronger now and heard a hissing sound. She looked overhead to see tendrils of flame spreading along the floorboards. Something dense fell through the hole, round balls of burning something, plopped onto the basement carpet, and sizzling there.

"What the hell was that?" Delores leaned closer, peering at the burning substance.

"Is that sap?" she muttered, looking back at the ceiling, then at the floor again, watching the mounds harden and turn black as she watched. More flaming balls fell through the ever-widening holes in her floor. She gasped again as she heard the basement door crack in two.

"GARY!" Delores screamed as she turned to flee the basement. "GARY!" She grabbed the basement door and flung it open, running wildly into the night.

She never knew what hit her as they snatched her head straight off her flailing body as she rounded the garage door. Her body toppled to the ground, twitching and kicking Lucille's tires as the car, and their neighborhood, burned.

Chapter 6

Jailhouse Rock

THE INVADERS REGROUPED IN the cul-de-sac, having made quick work of the warm bodies they had found. Smoke rose from every house on the street as fires burned. Green lawns smoldered under gobs of magma. Trails of lava and blood were all that remained as the horde of giant arachnids moved on toward a new scent, and the promise of more food. In the distance, fire and ash still spit from the rumbling volcano, still spewing living fireballs over the side and into the sea.

Three miles outside of town, sat the county jail, Potter's County pen, as it was fondly called, housed forty-three inmates for their short-term stays, and was manned by fifteen full-time staff, with a few part-timers that filled in as needed. Warden Jones was very proud of his jail and kept it running on a tight schedule. *"Ship-Shape"* as he often liked to say whenever asked. *"A good captain runs a tight ship and keeps it ship-shape."* Then he would grin, offer a firm handshake, and pat the reporter on the back for a job well done. The man loved to be interviewed about his jail. His ego only outshone his arrogance.

Tonight, he was fast asleep in his office, deciding to stay over so he could prepare for tomorrow's interview. It was a big day for him. Ten years as warden without a single incident, no deaths (other than natural causes, of course), no riots, no brawls. His prison was a shining example of hard work and rehabilitation. And he was being honored for it! Warden Jones, being honored by the mayor, no less.

As the Warden slept, snug in his bed, dreaming of keys to the city and big speeches, a wriggling mass of smoldering black bounded over the prison fence, over the gate, down the driveway, and right up to the concrete walls of the jail. The cell windows sat high on each wall, with bars attached to each one. The building was gray, squat, and drab, two stories in a square U-shape, with the exercise yard in the middle. The administrative offices sat closest to the main doors, with the wardens' private quarters just beyond the office wing. The mass of writhing organisms wasted no time launching their dense bodies at the glass, shattering windows, and crashing through the doors, skittering inside.

Their eyestalks flopped on their heads, twitching, and rotating wildly, scanning for warm bodies. The red eyes glowed brightly in the near total darkness. Lights flashed on across the compound as the guards woke up to the sounds of chaos and the siren blared. They quickly devoured the guards at the first desk as more of the spiders burst through their glass enclosure. One half-chewed head rolled and bounced down the hall before being snatched up by the jaws of another arachnid. They jammed into the small space; wriggling, chewing, blazing monsters intent on eating every living thing they found.

They began swarming down the halls; alarms blared, and lights flashed. Guards rushed toward the commotion, guns aimed, only to turn tail and run when they faced the monstrosities barreling toward them on skittering legs. Two of the braver guards got several shots fired, but they bounced harmlessly off the mass of hungry beasts coming towards them. Their screams only lasted seconds as the swarm engulfed and devoured them. A spray of blood, and a torn black boot, the only sign they had been there at all.

The cell doors all clanged open at once as the fleeing guards hit buttons and levers, trying to give the inmates a fighting chance, even as they were trying to flee into the madness. The noise was deafening in C block as the mass infiltrated the small rooms, knocking bodies down, chewing and tearing their way through the cowering humanity within.

Warden Jones awoke to the sirens and a loud ruckus coming from the administrative offices. He sat up groggily, a sour expression on his face, and plonked his wire lenses on his nose, yawning noisily.

"What in the hell is all that noise?" he muttered, already preparing the stern lecture he was going to give to whomever was causing the disruption. He jammed his legs into his trousers, donned a shirt, and shoved his feet into his shoes, sans socks, and blundered out into the hall.

Red emergency lights were strobing at the far end of the corridor. A scent of smoke and something rancid wafted past his nose and he wrinkled it in disgust.

"What is that god awful smell?" he said. "Guards!" He yelled out, "Johnson! Peters! Where are you?"

He blinked at the red lights that were more bobbing than strobing. They were at the wrong height somehow. His brain itched, trying to figure out what was wrong with the emergency lights.

"That's not right.... not right at all." He muttered to himself, then called out again. "Guards!" W*here in the world are they?* When he caught up with them, there would be hell to pay.

The warden strode forward down the hallway, nearing the glass door separating him from the offices, when it suddenly shattered.

The massive spiders began pouring into the hallway, lava oozing and sliding down their scurrying frames, red eyes bobbing and twirling as they focused on the warm meal just ahead of them.

Jones felt his bowels turn to water and then his balls shriveled so far up inside him, he wondered if he would ever find them again. He turned, piss leaking down his leg, as the creatures bounded toward him.

Two caught up with him, four legs skewering him from both ends. Warden Jones did not scream for long as his head disappeared with a sudden bite from razor-sharp teeth.

Lava dripped onto the stump of his neck as a second spider chewed on his legs, yanking the twitching body into its month, one bite at a time. Dozens of the spiders swarmed the hallways, spilling into offices, seeking any flesh they missed. Thin tendrils of fine orange webbing drifted from them as they went, coating everything it touched. It shimmered and swayed with the light breeze.

The cell blocks descended into carnage as the inmates huddled under cots, ran down halls, hid in the showers, and headed for the exits. The spiders were everywhere in the darkness. Glowing red eyes, smoldering flames, and strobing lights from the outside provided the only illumination as blood painted the walls. Trails of fire burned everywhere the spiders went, trailing behind them like contrails from hell, made from each mound of lava that oozed from their massive bodies.

The creatures surged up the stairs to the next level, seeking and eating as they went, cell by cell. The jailhouse was decimated as they consumed every bit of meat they found, and their flames consumed the rest.

Jonas Taylor slipped from his cot in his small room behind the kitchen. His old bones creaked in protest as he stood up and reached for his robe. Something awful was happening out there. If his thirty years in the system had taught him anything, it was to mind his business. He was not about to go see what it was. He grabbed his personal items, stuffed them in his small knapsack, and then, clad only in his socks, robe, and pajamas, he snuck quietly into the hallway and headed toward the kitchen exit.

He knew the jail better than anyone, and his plan of escape was the kitchen delivery dock. He had the key. The sounds of screaming echoed distantly as he kept his eyes on the door ahead.

"Not today, Satan. No, sir. Not today." He muttered, taking care not to bump into anything as he went. He could smell the flames, smelled the ripe scent of blood. He did *not* want to see any more than he wanted to hear.

Old Jonas kept going, skittering down the hall in his socks almost as fast as the creatures wreaking havoc in the cell blocks. *"Got to go call someone. Get the police in here. The National Guard. Hell, Anyone will do."* He muttered under his breath, *"That's what I'm going to do. Ain't playing no hero today, Lord."*

The old man reached his exit, slid the key into the lock, and exhaled in relief as the fresh night air filled his nostrils. He stepped outside, down the steps, and fled into the night. The opposite direction of the jail and Blueberry Hill, toward the hospital just beyond the next hill.

Chapter 7

Oh, What A Night!

Dr. Jamison stepped outside of the Emergency Room exit, inhaling the night air. He normally loved working nights in the quiet town, right above the coastline, where nothing ever happened. Broken arms and sunburn, Band-Aids, and castor oil. But tonight, something foul was in the air, or maybe in the water, he thought snidely, a smirk on his face. Several residents had come in, screaming hysterically about giant spiders and flaming rocks. Weird burns were on some of them, others only blood-spattered and shell-shocked. They looked like they had been through war, not simply downtown on Main street.

Three teens had staggered in from the drive-in, sobbing about a massacre and space invaders, fireballs, and black blobs. They were missing shoes; one was missing his shirt. The girl said they had walked here all the way through the woods. He couldn't make sense of most of what they said. The girl had two puncture wounds on her leg that looked like someone had cauterized immediately them after. The oldest boy was missing half his arm. He was already in shock when Jamison had reached him. The other was uninjured, physically at least. His mental state was another story. He sedated all three after treating their wounds and had admitted them.

Parents had been called, but he got no answer at any of the homes. He had left a note for the nurses to try again. He expected hysterical phone calls from mothers at any moment, considering it was approaching three in the morning and the drive-in ended at midnight. What mother was not waiting up on her teenager to come home from the movies?

He sighed and rubbed his eyes, watching the weird orange glow over the mountain. That was strange for sure. He could swear the ground was rumbling ever so slightly beneath his feet. He stretched then, arching his back just a little with his hands over his head, trying to loosen the knots. A night full of crazy had him tense and sore.

"Oh, what a night." He sighed again, one hand rubbing at a deep knot in his neck.

The breeze kicked up, and he inhaled deeply, relishing the clean air, but then he coughed. Tears poured from his eyes. Smoke was thick in the air, drifting from somewhere nearby. Not a clean smoke, like a campfire, but something rancid clung to it. Unclean smells of sulfur and ash, like something rotten rode the undercurrent as he coughed and retched. Finally able to breathe normally, he took shallow breaths through his mouth and turned in a slow circle, watching the dark sky above.

He couldn't see smoke, but he could smell it growing stronger. There were more lights glimmering through the trees, orange and red shimmering dots of light. It was almost like he could see the traffic lights from the main road, but that couldn't be it. But they were flickering from orange to red and back, bobbing and weaving in the distance, like a breeze making the hanging lights dance on their cables.

He squinted toward the back of the emergency parking lot. He thought he saw movement just beyond the edge of the lot.

He watched for a moment, concentrating on the dark spot where he thought he saw the motion, and a second later, a man emerged from the shadows. An old man, shuffling along in dingy white socks, and a ratty bathrobe. He was dark-skinned and had tufts of white hair sticking up on his almost bald head. The man looked up and saw him, waved frantically, then broke into a faster shuffle.

"Hey! Hey, Doc! Hey." the man yelled.

Jamison lifted one hand in a wave, watching him approach, a wary expression on his face.

"Is everything okay, sir?" He asked, eyeing the old man as he caught his breath.

"No, sir. No sir, it ain't." the man wheezed, hands on his knees as he panted and huffed. "Call the cops, man! Call everyone! Call the Army, the Navy! The National Guard! Get them down here, now!"

The man rasped, turning to drop to the stairs, sitting hard on the concrete and leaning against the rail. "Something bad happened over at the jail. There's fire everywhere and blood all in the air." He sobbed, his voice quavering as he told the tale.

"Blood? In the air?" the doctor said, one eyebrow raised as he looked at the old man. "What do you mean, blood in the air?"

"Blood, man! Blood. I can smell it. I've been to war. Been in prison. I know blood when I smell it. And that jail is thick with it. Blood and fire raining down over there. You gotta call someone, Doc. Please!" Jonas clutched at the doc's hand, pleading with him.

"Alright, now, alright. Just calm down. Let's get you inside and get you warm. I'll see who I can call. We've already called the Sheriff, but we can't raise anyone down there."

"Call the next county over, Doc. Try again, they're coming! Oh god, they're coming for us all!"

"Come now, calm yourself, man!" Dr. Jamison offered the old man his hand and helped him up. "Let's get you inside. It's been a long night."

"It's about to get longer, Doc." Old Jonas said as they went inside. He took one last look behind him and his eyes widened as he saw bobbing lights in the distance growing closer by the second.

"Better hurry up that phone call, Doc."

"What?" Jamison turned to him once more and followed where he pointed. An orange glow was emerging from the woods, red glowing dots hovered just over it. Not a row of red, but a dancing sea of spots of red, all moving and twisting at once.

"What the hell is that?" Jamison said, forgetting all about getting Jonas safely inside.

"*That* is what I don't want to find out." Jonas said. "Get to a phone, now!" He pushed the doctor inside and stepped in after him. He locked the door as it swung shut. His stomach churned and sour bile rose in his throat. That lock would not keep this nightmare out. Old Jonas trusted his gut. It had kept him alive this long. He turned and followed the doctor to the nurse's station. He was determined to see him make that phone call. Then, he was slipping out of the nearest exit and as far away from here as he could get.

Chapter 8

What'd I Say?

"HOLD ON NOW, DOC. What's that you say?" Deputy Smithers said into the phone. "Fires at the jail? I see." He jotted down a note as he listened to the voice on the other end once more. "No response from your guys over there. No, I don't think the National Guard is needed." Smithers smirked as he listened again, shaking his head. "I got it, sure, sure. I'll send a few guys right over and try to ring the sheriff for you again." Another long pause while the other voice continued; Smithers rolled his eyes at Roy, watching him from behind his desk. "Alright, doc. Have a good night. I'm sure it's nothing. See you soon."

Smithers hung up and tapped his pencil on the notepad he held. "Boy, I tell ya, what a crazy call."

"What's going on?" Roy asked.

"This Doc Jamison from up in Pine Grove, yelling about a massacre at the jail, a big fire too, and some other nut in the background talking nonsense about fireballs and things coming from the woods." Smithers chuckled, then picked up the phone.

"Well, are you going to go up there or not?" Roy said, raising an eyebrow.

"We have to go check it out." Smithers said with a shrug. "We can go soon as I try to ring the sheriff over there for them. The doc said he's been trying to call, but no one is answering the telephone."

"Alright. I'll go get the car." Roy stood up, eager to have something to do. It had been a long and boring night and he was ready for some fresh air. Besides, how bad could it be? It sounded like a bunch of rubbish, anyway. He could use a drive.

Roy ambled out of the police station, as Smithers tried to ring the Pine Grove police station once more.

A few minutes later, Smithers walked outside and got in the car with Roy, still shaking his head, equally amused and perplexed.

"Well?" Roy asked as he got in.

"No luck." his partner said, "It's the damnedest thing. No response at the station or at his residence. No luck at the firehouse either. It's like they're all gone."

"Maybe they are already on the call?" Roy offered helpfully as he steered the car out of town.

"Maybe. I called Sheriff Hicks too and asked him to send a few of the others out just in case. We can radio him when we get to Potter's. After we see what is going on over there."

"Good idea. I was ready for a drive, anyway." Roy replied, stifling a bored yawn as he flicked on the lights and sirens. His inner child never tired of flipping that switch. He grinned as he pushed the gas down harder.

"Easy there, cowboy." Smithers chuckled. "I'm sure there's no need to speed."

Roy only smiled, happy to be away from the station for any reason.

"There, are you happy? I called." Doc Jamison said to Jonas as the old man stood shuffling back and forth in front of him. "They are going to call the sheriff and send a couple of men out to check out the jail. When they get here, you can tell them what you saw."

"It's gonna be too late for that, doc." Jonas said, still pacing in his socks. He clutched a cup of coffee in his hands, trying to stop his shaking.

"Look, you've had a scare. You're upset. Why don't I get you settled in a room? You can rest here tonight while we sort out the jail situation and figure things out in the morning." Dr. Jamison said, keeping his tone soothing despite his own frustration. Nothing was making any sense tonight. It was as if the entire town had gone mad.

"No, thanks, doc. If it's all the same to you, I'm just going to be on my way now. Thank you for the coffee and for making that phone call. It's time for me to go. I suggest you do the same." Jonas set the cup down on the desk and began shuffling toward the main entrance.

"Jonas, wait." Jamison called after him. "You don't have shoes on or any proper clothes. You can go out like that."

"Why not? I got here like this." Jonas chuckled. "I got to go now, Doc. I really think you should come with me."

THUD! THUD! THUD!

Both men froze as a loud noise echoed down the hallway. Jamison turned toward the Emergency Room, trying to see down the darkened hall.

"Time to go, Doc." Jonas trudged away, down an opposite hallway.

"What was that?" The doctor said,

"*That* means it's time to go." the old man replied, not slowing his pace. "*That* is what got in the jail and *that* is what came out of the woods. I know you saw those lights. *Their* lights."

Jamison never noticed when Jonas disappeared down the long corridor. He was too focused on the hovering and twisting red lights just outside of the emergency room.

CRASH!

Jonas ducked around the corner, followed another short hallway, then took a left, found the stairs, followed those down, and took another left. He had no plan other than to find an exit that led in the opposite direction of the emergency room. He felt bad for all the poor patients in their beds, but he couldn't help them. The best he could do was try to save himself. A terrified scream echoed down the halls as whatever *it* was caught up to Dr. Jamison. He trudged along faster, tying his bathrobe a bit more snugly around his waist. As he reached the end of the corridor, he snagged a crutch from a pair that stood forgotten in a corner and took it with him. *Better than no weapon at all*, he thought.

He spied an exit up ahead of him and kept his eyes on the doorway. The floor above him rumbled and several patients shrieked in tandem. *"Lord, help them. I sure can't."* He muttered, reaching the doorway, and peering out of it for a long moment, looking for any sign of danger before he pushed the latch down and opened it wide. He stuck his head out and scanned the area again.

He must be near the cafeteria as small groups of picnic tables were scattered in the grassy space before him. Several flower beds lined the walkways between them. No lights. No reds. No orange glow. He stepped outside and hurried away, back to the trees, and hopefully, to safety. Old Jonas said a silent prayer for the souls of the patients as he left them screaming in the dark.

Deputy Roy eased the car up to Potter's Jail, mouth dropping open at the scene before him. Smithers sat beside him, stunned at the condition of the jailhouse. The fences were bent and twisted. Windows were smashed, doors wrenched from their frames, and flames still poured from inside. Smithers reached for the radio.

"Sheriff Hicks, come in, Smithers here."

"Go head, Smithers, Hicks here." Came the static-filled reply.

"Um, we're here at Potter's and it's on fire. Just like the doc said. You're going to want to come up here."

"On fire? Are the inmates loose? Where are the guards?" Hicks asked.

"No guards found. No warden. No police. No one. Send help." Smithers answered, his voice rising in pitch as a tinge of fear entered it.

"Roy." Smithers said, eyes widening.

"Roy!"

"What?" his partner asked, ducking his head back inside the car.

"What is that?" Smithers pointed to a round shape rolling around the edge of the building.

Roy straightened up and looked to where Smithers had pointed. There were three of the weird balls now, smoldering like they were on fire, a weird orange glow emanating from within them.

"What the hell is that?"

Smithers got back on the radio as the glowing orbs unfurled. Bright red eyes popped up and began rotating and scanning. A dozen eyes suddenly focused on them at the same time. More of the rolling balls appeared from inside the building as the ones in front took shape. The massive bodies of the spiders rose to full height and their black legs skittered full tilt toward the police car.

Roy pulled his gun and fired, backing away with every shot. Smithers screamed into the radio. "Call the National Guard! Call the Army! Call Everyone! Now!"

"What is going on out there?" Hicks demanded.

"What'd I say, man? Get help. Call Washington! Call in the big guns!" Smithers screamed. "They're spiders, man! Giant fucking spiders made of fire and smoke! Get help, now! Get out here!" Smithers dropped the radio, grabbed his firearm, and took aim, shooting right through the windshield as the first of many pounced on the hood.

Roy emptied his gun and fled toward the road. The skittering sound behind him made his stomach churn and his skull ache. The air was thick with ash and smoke; tears poured from his eyes as he ran, struggling to breathe and trying to see through the pre-dawn smoky haze. He didn't see the spider rising in front of him until its front legs shot through his chest, skewering him where he stood.

His eyes rolled up as blood trickled from his mouth. The last thing Deputy Roy ever saw was the needle-sharp teeth of the monster closing around his head, Smither's screams echoing in what was left of his mind.

As Roy's body dropped, headless, to the pavement, Smithers bolted from the car, narrowly missing a barbed leg shooting through the windshield. A brown stain was spreading on the back of his trousers as piss streamed down his leg. He barely felt it as he took off toward the trees behind the jail. The things followed him, dozens of legs skittering in tandem as they pursued him. He raced around the edge of the ruined jailhouse and into the exercise yard, cussing as he tripped. He tried to regain his balance and slipped into something wet.

Smithers went down hard, hands sliding through a congealing puddle of blood and gore. Chunks of organs and tissue clung to his hands. He sat up quickly, flinging the mess from his hands, screaming like a little girl as the spiders swarmed him. His cries for his mommy were the last words he ever said as bits of his own tissue and gore rained down on the concrete.

A half-dozen spiders consumed him, snarling, and tearing his limbs and torso to bits, consuming everything except his shoes. When their meal was finished, they moved away into the trees to rejoin the rest of their kin. They had found a new scent. A new meal waited just beyond the forest.

Sheriff Hicks hung up the phone and headed for the door, his sweaty face bright red with anger. Two of his deputies followed him. "What'd they say, boss?" Deputy Anthony asked him, the eager young rookie of the force.

"Well, what do you think they said?" Hicks asked rather snidely. "They laughed me right off the phone. Giant spiders! For chrissakes. Fucking National Guard, my ass." He spat furiously.

"What do you think happened then?" Anthony asked again.

"Anthony. When we get there, I will tell you. Until then, shut your trap and get in the car."

Anthony nodded, red in the face, and hurried to get into his car.

Hicks and Davis got into the other car, and they sped off toward Potter's County Pen. The scent of smoke was heavy in the air and Hicks felt like a ball of lead had just taken up residence in his gut. He pushed the gas harder and gripped the wheel, mentally steeling himself for whatever he was speeding toward.

Chapter 9
Good golly, Miss Molly!

OLD JONAS MADE HIS way through the trees, using the wooden crutch as a walking stick and a scythe, whacking branches and vines out of his way as he went. The old man was bloodied, sore, and tired. His arms, face, and feet all bore scratches and cuts from his flights into the forest, but he kept going. He knew the county line was just around the bend and he had stuck parallel to the road. He could see it faintly, a flat gray patch just beyond the trees. Tears leaked from his eyes, and he made no move to wipe them away. There had been good men at the jail, most there for petty crimes, many of them had been his friends.

The doctor had seemed to be kind as well and Jonas felt right terrible about what had happened. *Whatever had happened.* He did not want to know, even now. He saw enough to know that it was all bad and nothing he wanted to have in his head for the rest of his days. He shook his head, unconsciously agreeing with his inner thoughts. His chest ached with sorrow, unshed sobs, but now was not the time.

He would get someone to listen to him, even if it was the last thing he did on this earth. Jonas glanced at the sky once more, breathing a sigh of relief. Dawn would break soon. The first streaks of gray light were peaking over the treetops. He hurried his steps a bit, eager to get to a house, or a building. Anywhere that might have a phone, or a person left alive inside it.

WHACK! THWACK!

He swung the crutch right and left, battling back a large bramble. He swore as one branch snapped back and caught his cheek, ripping it open as it slid along the lined flesh. He swiped at the blood with one hand and kept going. His crutch swung with every step, and he closed his mind to the burning pain in his feet.

The lives lost tonight had endured worse. He would endure this. Jonas took a deep breath and pushed through, praying with every step he took that someone would come, that someone was left.

Molly Pettigrew stepped out of her house, a steaming cup of coffee in one hand. She loved this time of morning. Just before dawn, the world was quiet, and she could just breathe in the peace. She took in washing for many of her elderly neighbors and liked to get an early start. That way she had all afternoon to starch, iron, fold, and deliver them in pristine, laundered condition.

She brought the coffee to her nose and inhaled deeply, loving the roasted aroma, the crisp scent of burning wood... *wait, burning what?* She inhaled again. Yep, still smoke. She set the cup on the railing and stepped off the porch, gazing up into the sky.

Sure enough, just over the hills, smoke was wafting over the treetops. Several thick tendrils of smoke curled up in multiple places, darker in some spots. "I wonder what's on fire over there." She said to herself, turning to her left to scan the horizon. *It all seems to be coming from Pine Grove,* she thought. *I better go call the sheriff, just in case. I don't hear any sirens.*

Molly stepped back onto her porch, forgetting all about her coffee, curious about what was going on but determined to find out. She left her front door open as she hastened to the kitchen.

When the dispatcher took her call, Molly quickly explained what she saw. She waited while they took down her name and address, then asked if there was any information on what was going on.

"I see. And you don't know when Sheriff Hicks will be back?" She waited for the response, impatiently tapping her foot.

"A fire at the jail? Oh my. I see. Well, alright then. Please have him call me when he gets back."

Another pause while the dispatcher replied, more foot tapping and lip biting.

"Alright, well, thank you. Goodbye." Molly hung up, not satisfied with the information, but there was nothing she could do. She had done her duty.

She leaned against the kitchen counter, biting her lip once more, then spied her coffee pot. *Ah, yes, my coffee!*

Molly remembered she left her mug on the front porch and headed toward the door to retrieve it. Just as she reached the door, she saw two things almost at the same time.

A massive glowing spider was hovering just at her front steps, and an old man was rushing it, with a wooden crutch held like a ball bat.

THWACK! THWACK! THWACK!

He swung again and again, screaming all the while as he battled it back from her front steps.

"Get Inside!" He yelled. "Git Inside!"

Molly did not need to be told twice. She backed away and slammed the door, locking it, then dragging a chair over to block it. She raced to the window to see what was happening.

The old man was still beating the creature with the crutch. The thing was thrusting its two front legs at him, trying to get past the crutch to his flesh, but he was quick on his feet.

THWACK! THWACK!

SQUEEEE! SQUEEEE!

The spider squealed in the highest pitch Molly had ever heard. She clasped her ears to block the sound, grimacing in pain as the battle outside continued.

SQUEEE! SQUEEEE! SQUEEE!

THWACK!

Molly dropped to her knees, gasping, feeling liquid trickle from her ears. She moved one hand to check and saw that it was bloody. She scooted backwards across the carpet, still clutching her ears. She made it across the room to the closet and crawled inside, huddling in the corner, trembling.

The chaos outside continued. Molly felt her fear recede in concern for the old man fighting for his life on her lawn. How could she just hide in here? Daddy had taught her better than that. She opened the door, and lurched to her feet, feeling around the top shelf for her Daddy's' old rifle.

Her hands closed around the cold metal, and she snagged it, dragging it forward until she could lift it with both hands. She brought it down and leaned it against the wall. *Shells. Where were those damn shells?* She stretched up on her tiptoes, feeling around for them, swiping hats and scarves aside. *There!* She grabbed the box, set it down on the table beside her, and loaded the chambers of the shotgun.

"Help me! Someone, please help!" The old man screamed for help outside.

Molly steeled herself, pumped the shotgun, and flung open the front door. Blood trickled from both her ears.

"Move!" she yelled at him, watching him stagger backwards as the skittering spider took another jab at him.

KABOOM!

Molly fired. The creature shrieked and turned on her. Lava poured through the new hole in its round body.

KABOOM!

She fired once more, aiming right for the top of its head. A chunk of its head sheared right off, taking half of its eyes with it. It shrieked, spinning in a crazy circle, then took off drunkenly down the road, falling and leaning like it could no longer navigate.

SQUEEEE! SQUEEEE!

The screeching continued long after it had vanished into the murky woods.

Molly walked over to the old man and helped him up.

"Thank you, Miss. Thank you so much! We gotta call for help! There's more of those things out there. We gotta warn someone!" He sobbed as she led him to the steps to sit down.

"I already called the sheriff, but he's out on a call."

"I know. Doc Jamison called him too. But them things got him. They got in the jailhouse too." He sniffed. "But we still need more help. There are hundreds of them out there."

"What's your name, sir?" She asked, helping him back to his feet.

"Jonas, Ma'am. Jonas Taylor."

"It's very nice to meet you, Jonas. I'm Molly. Now let's go make some calls. My Daddy happens to be an Admiral in the Navy." She smiled. "He will know just what to do."

Jonas sniffed back another sob as they went up the steps. He still held his crutch. Molly held her daddy's shotgun at the ready as he limped inside. He just hoped they weren't too late to save the rest of the town.

Made in the USA
Columbia, SC
31 August 2023

22320620R00036